S0-BYE-967

Tiger on a Tree

Anushka Ravishankar

Pulak Biswas

TARA PUBLISHING

Tiger, tiger

on the shore

Does he war

o go across?

Make a dash?

Be bold? Be rash?

splash!

Tiger, tiger,

going far

Baaaaaaaa

Yaaaaaaa

aaah!

This tree is the

only place to be!

Tiger!

Tiger?

On a tree!

Tiger? On a tree?

Rubbish! Cannot be

It's true! I saw it too!

Now what to do?

Get him! Net him!

Tie him tight!

Will he bite?

He might!

Shoo him!

Boo him!

Make him jump!

Dum duma dum dum

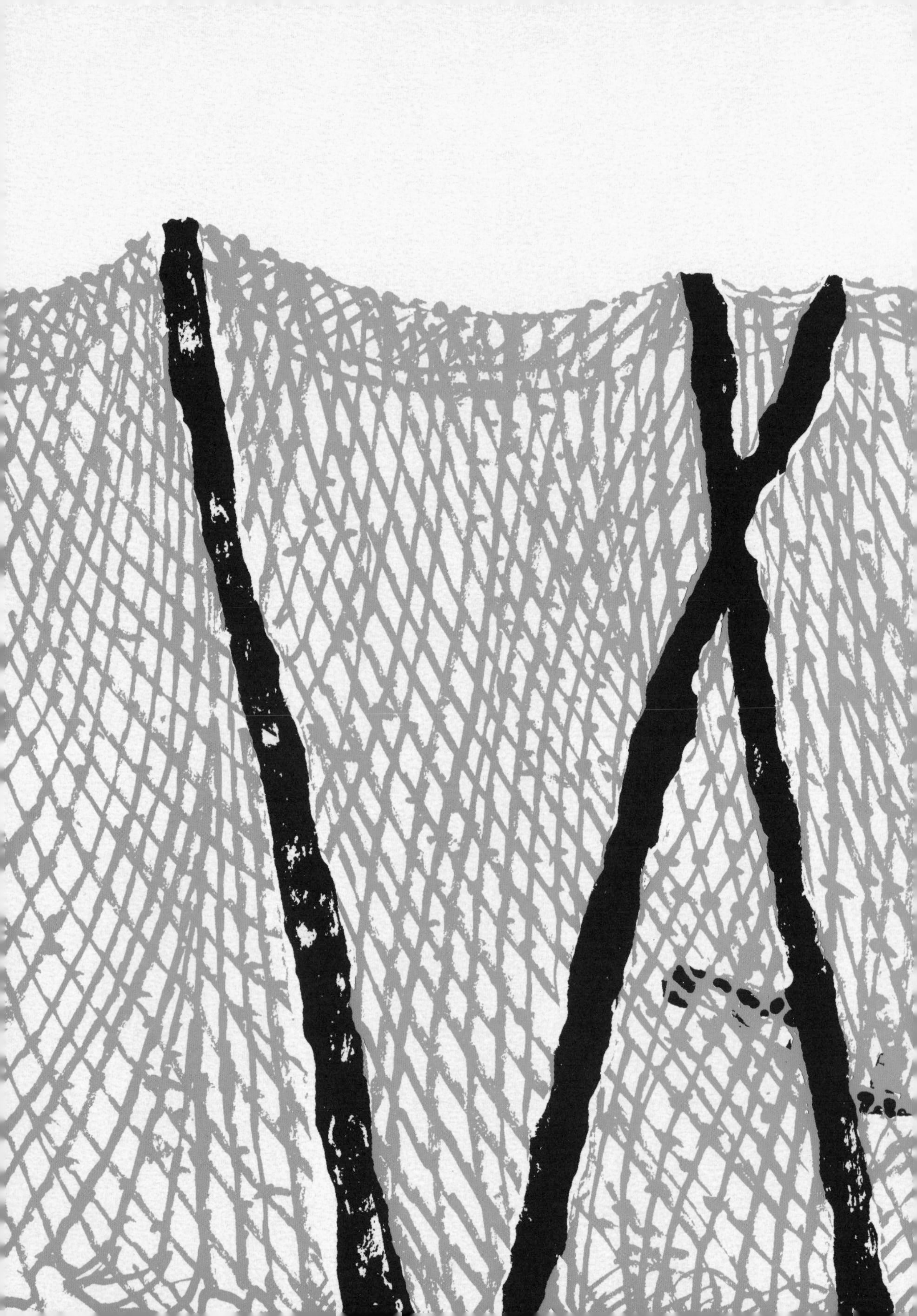

Thump.

He's caught. He's got.

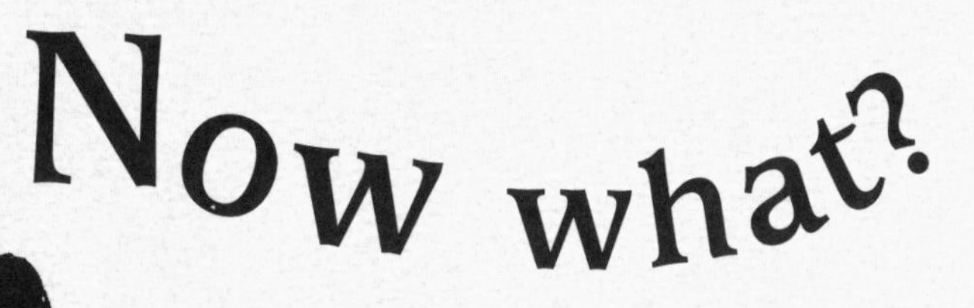
Now what?

Send him to the ZOO?

Stick him up with glue?

Paint him an electric blue?

I know, set him free.

Free???

Yes!
Yes!

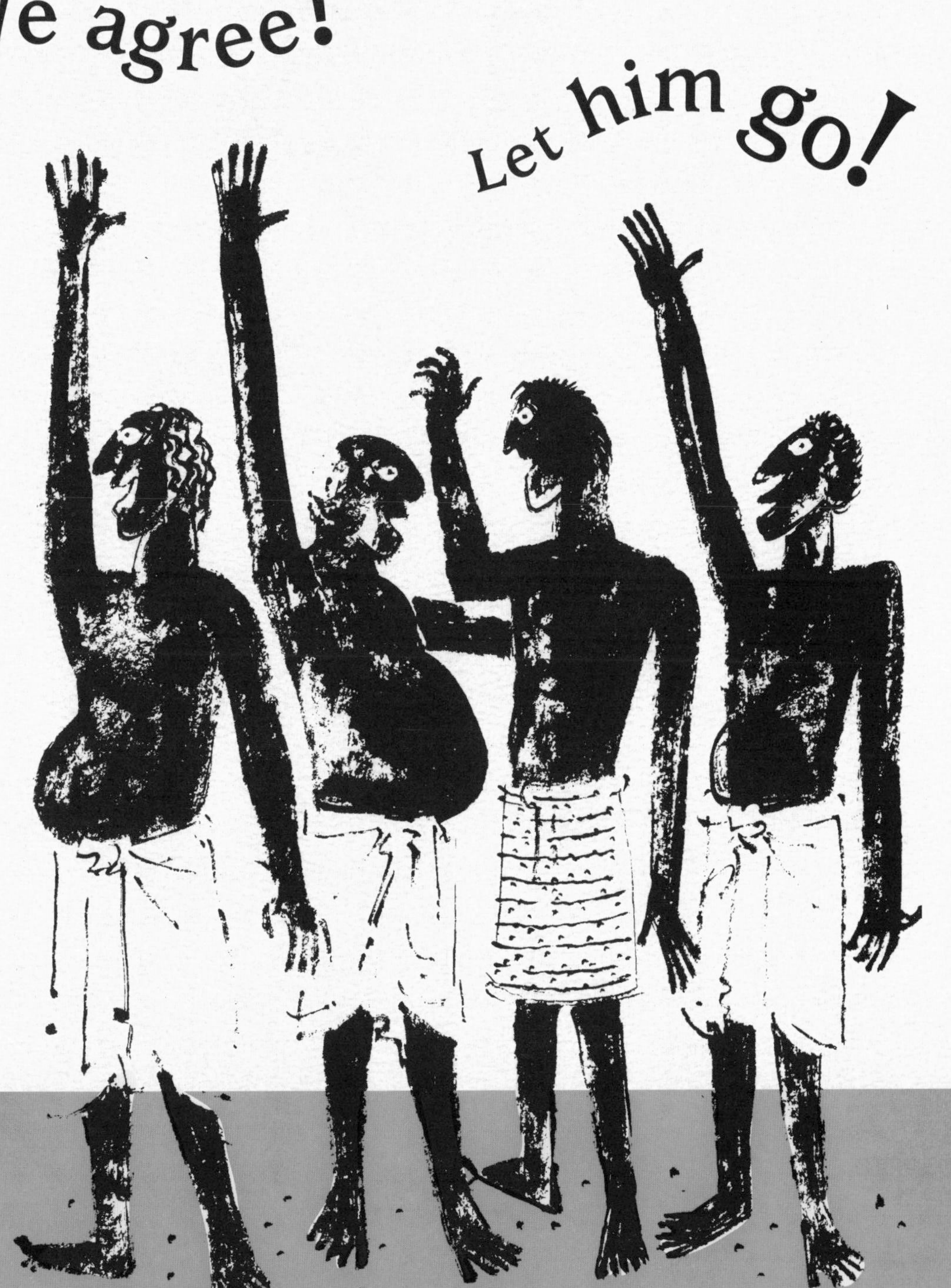
We agree!
Let him go!

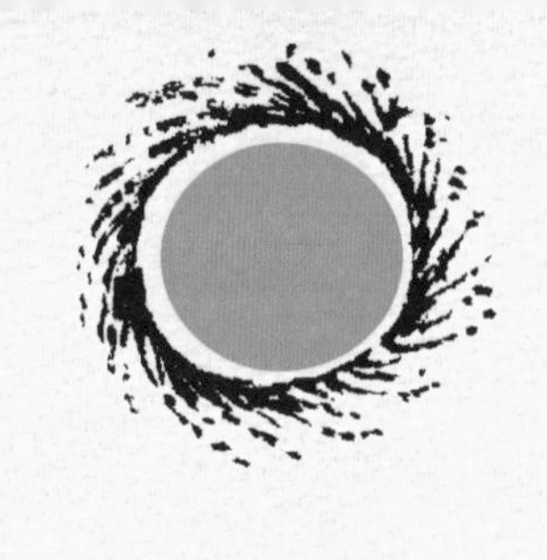

So.

Tiger, tiger on the shore

Tiger on a Tree

Copyright © 1997

For the text: Anushka Ravishankar
For the illustrations: Pulak Biswas

For this edition:
Tara Publishing Ltd., UK < www.tarabooks.com/uk >
and
Tara Publishing, India < www.tarabooks.com >

First printed 1997, Reprinted 2002, 2004, this offset edition 2007

Design: Rathna Ramanathan, Minus9 Design
Production: C. Arumugam
Printed in Thailand by Sirivatana Interprint PCL.

All rights reserved. No part of this work may be reproduced in any form without the prior written permission of the publisher

ISBN 978-81-86211-38-0